Robin Hood
A
Hidden Picture
Story

Retold and Illustrated by
Kit Wray

BELL
BOOKS

To Beth, Arlynn, and John

Copyright © 1992 by Kit Wray
All rights reserved
Published by Bell Books
Boyds Mills Press, Inc.
A Highlights Company
910 Church Street
Honesdale, Pennsylvania 18431

Publisher Cataloging-in-Publication Data
Wray, Kit.
    Robin Hood: a hidden picture fairy tale / retold and illustrated by Kit Wray.
    [32] p. : ill. ; cm.
Summary: Retells the adventures of Robin Hood and his band of men in Sherwood Forest.
Hidden pictures are found throughout the illustrations.
ISBN 1-56397-020-1
1. Robin Hood (Legendary character). [1. Robin Hood (Legendary Character),
2. Folklore—England.] I. Title.
398.22 / 0941—dc20   1992
Library of Congress Catalog Card Number: 91-72976
First edition, 1992
Distributed by St. Martin's Press
Printed in the United States of America

Many years ago, King Richard the Lion-Hearted of England left his throne to fight in the Crusades. Those who ruled in his absence treated the people of the land unfairly.

During this time there lived in the country near Sherwood Forest an able-bodied youth named Robin Hood. While journeying one day to Nottingham, where he hoped to see his fair Maid Marian, Robin passed a group of foresters. Seeing his bow, they began to taunt him.

Robin became angry and foolishly wagered he could strike a deer in the distance. At this the men laughed, but Robin quickly drew his bow, and in seconds the stag lay still.

"You have killed the King's deer!" the foresters cried. Realizing his mistake, Robin hastened toward the forest, but one of the men sent an arrow flying close by his ear. Robin turned and sped an answering shaft into the man's shoulder.

Thus did Robin Hood become an outlaw, and the Sheriff of Nottingham offered a high reward for his capture.

So Robin dwelt hidden in Sherwood Forest and greatly missed seeing Marian, for they had hoped to wed.

sailboat, baseball bat, sock, flute, horseshoe, parrot

There gathered about Robin other men who had been outlawed unjustly, among them valiant Will Scarlet. The men chose Robin for their chief. They fashioned clothing of dark green and built homes for themselves in the wild beauty of Sherwood.

Robin and his band won renown as skilled bowmen and brave fighters. They freely shared any goods they wrested from the rich and powerful with those who were oppressed.

light bulb, woodpecker, heads of a mouse, a collie, and a crow   3

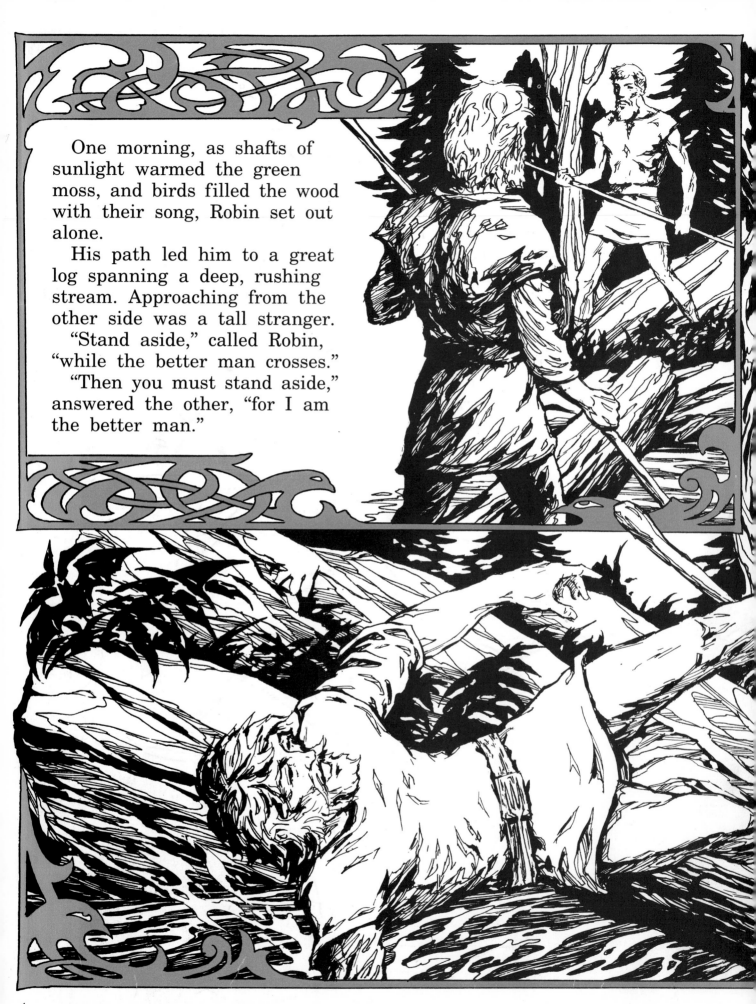

One morning, as shafts of sunlight warmed the green moss, and birds filled the wood with their song, Robin set out alone.

His path led him to a great log spanning a deep, rushing stream. Approaching from the other side was a tall stranger.

"Stand aside," called Robin, "while the better man crosses."

"Then you must stand aside," answered the other, "for I am the better man."

heads of a goose and an ape, pointing hand, bat, fork, witch's hat

Noticing the strong staff the stranger held, Robin said, "Wait while I cut a staff to match yours."

Then both men stepped onto the log. As the water swirled below them, the two began to spar. Many a strong blow was parried by the other's staff.

Robin dealt the stranger a whack on the ribs, but the stranger held his balance and swung his own staff squarely aside Robin's head.

Robin was hurled from the log, and he struck the water with a great splash.

As Robin surfaced, the stranger roared with laughter. Robin clambered upon the bank, all soaked and dripping with weeds, and laughed aloud at himself.

Then he raised his horn to his lips and sent forth a blast that echoed through the forest. Soon his green-clad men emerged from the shadows.

"Yonder stranger has given me a lesson in the cudgel I shall not forget," said Robin. "What is your name, friend?"

"I am called John Little," replied the stranger.

"I shall call you 'Little John' instead. I am Robin Hood. If you join our band, you will be my right-hand man and share our merry life in Sherwood."

6   mouse, arrow, pie, banana, dog's head, mushroom

The Sheriff of Nottingham, meanwhile, was plotting how he might capture Robin Hood. At last he sent messengers to every hamlet in the countryside, proclaiming a great shooting match to be held in Nottingham. Anyone who could draw a longbow was bidden to compete for the prize of a golden arrow. The Sheriff prepared his men to seize Robin should the outlaw be tempted to come show his skill.

hammer, rabbit, butterfly, boomerang, suitcase, funnel

When the day of the match arrived, merchants, pages, and knights with their ladies all gathered around the target range outside the town walls. On a raised seat beneath colored banners sat the Sheriff.

heads of an elephant and a chipmunk, folding knife, dragonfly, squirrel, axe

After the trumpets had sounded, each competitor shot in turn.

Then everyone laughed as a tattered beggar stepped forward with his bow. He was dressed in scarlet and wore a patch over one eye. Taking a shaft from his quiver, he looked over at Maid Marian. All fell silent as he drew his bow, held it a moment, and then released the arrow. Dead center it lodged as the onlookers stared in amazement.

"Receive your prize," grumbled the Sheriff when the beggar came before him. The scarlet stranger then walked over to Maid Marian and silently handed her the arrow. Their eyes met, and she nodded and smiled. He turned and walked boldly off the field.

hammer, heads of an eagle and a goose, broom, spoon, horn   9

That night the Sheriff sat at meat with his men. "I had expected to catch Robin Hood at the match today," he said. "But who was that insolent beggar who shot so well?"

Just then an arrow flew through the window and lodged in the table with a thud. There was a scroll attached to its shaft. When the Sheriff read the note, he trembled with rage.

It read—

"Greetings to Your Grace, from Sherwood. You have given the prize to Robin Hood."

kite, mug, slice of bread, buckle, envelope, accordion

Several days later Robin wandered through the country dressed in chain mail with a sword by his side. On the banks of a wide stream, he came upon a stout friar.

"Ho," said Robin. "Would one so strong as you be willing to carry me across this stream? I would not have this steel tunic go to rust."

Chuckling to himself, the friar took Robin upon his back and stepped into the ford.

"Lest your sword get wet," said the friar, "I will carry it."

glove, fish, seal, heads of a baboon and a duck   11

When Robin had been deposited on the other shore, he asked for his sword. Then he saw the friar's own broadsword beneath his brown robe.

"I'll not return your sword unless you carry me back from whence we came," laughed the jolly man.

But while Robin waded across with the smiling friar on his back, he secretly unfastened the other's sword belt. So when the friar was set down, it was Robin who brandished both swords.

"Now," said Robin, "if you would have your own blade again, be kind enough to carry me over this stream."

heads of a cat, a lamb, and a donkey, wrench, arrowhead, cane

This time, when the friar had carried Robin to the center of the stream, he pitched him over his shoulders into the deepest water.

Then began an earnest duel between the two, their broadswords clashing together until the sun was low.

At that time Robin raised his horn, and shortly a dozen of his band came running from the trees.

Then the friar blew upon his whistle, and four huge hounds burst from the thicket, with fangs bared.

pterodactyl, dog's head, duck, goldfish, spoon, pen

The good friar let forth peals of laughter as Robin and his men raced for the tallest trees.

"By the way," called Robin from his perch overhead, "I would be honored to have such a skilled swordsman in my band. I am Robin Hood."

"Good master! I have heard your name often. I am Friar Tuck." And with great apologies Friar Tuck called off his dogs as Robin descended the tree.

The friar gladly joined Robin's band that day.

feather, heart, drumstick, carrot, eel, lizard

The Sheriff was out hunting one evening when his path led him into Sherwood Forest. Suddenly he was surrounded by a dozen men in green, and Robin Hood stepped forward.

"Noble Sheriff, surely you have journeyed here to enjoy our hospitality!"

They led his horse to their home beneath the tall trees. Then, with merry smiles, they invited the grim-faced Sheriff to sit upon the moss. While the fires crackled, they served him the best fare they could muster and entertained him royally.

Robin said, "Before you return home, good Sheriff, we will gratefully accept your purse of gold."

crown, heads of a dog and a goat, trumpet, teacup, high-heeled shoe

When he returned to Nottingham, the Sheriff called his men-at-arms together and demanded to have Robin Hood captured at any cost. Several groups of soldiers hid themselves in different parts of the forest.

Robin chose Will Scarlet to learn where they were hiding. Will ventured out at dawn in a monk's robe that covered his heavy sword. He soon found a group of the Sheriff's soldiers at a country inn.

hoe, shark, rake, hat, pail

Will sat down far from their table and covered his face with his cowl. But a cat brushed his robe aside, exposing the gleaming sword.

One soldier called out, "When does a friar arm himself?" Will drew his weapon and smote the advancing soldier on his helm. But the rest set upon Will and wounded him sorely.

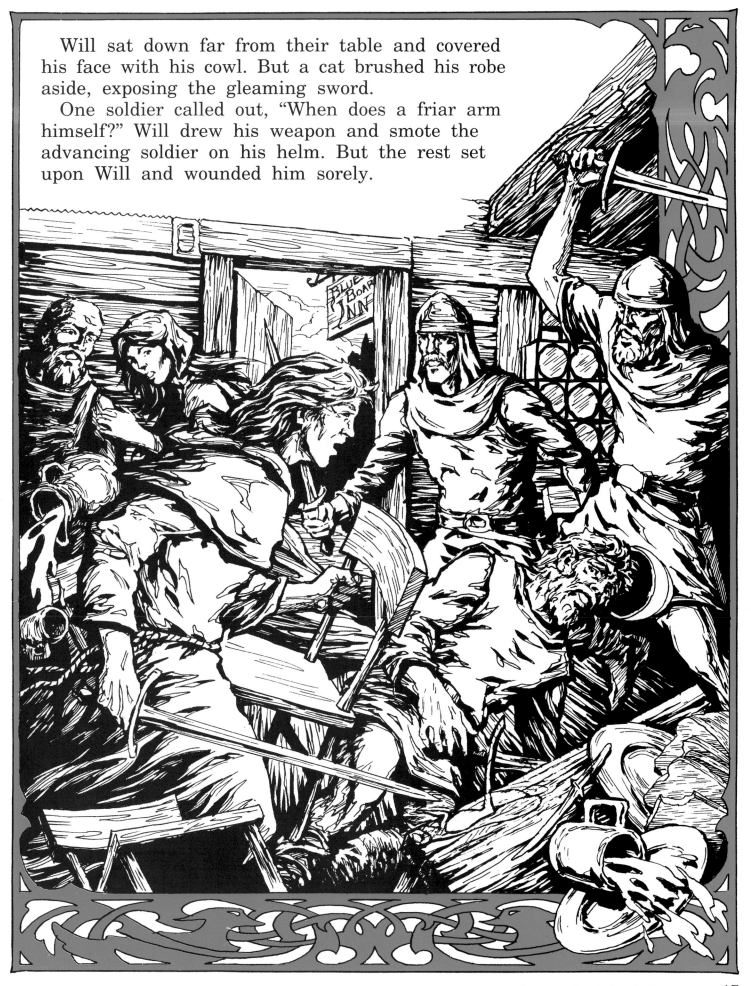

moon, saw, jump rope, grasshopper, giant's head, lantern

Robin was waiting for Will to return when he heard a horse pounding up the path toward him. "Marian!" cried Robin. The lady reined in her horse where Robin stood.

"I had to come," she answered. "They have taken Will Scarlet to the Sheriff's castle and will hang him tomorrow!"

"Thank you," said Robin. "We will be there. But get you gone before the Sheriff's men see you here."

ladybug, salamander, bow, ring, pancake flipper, heads of a wolf, a bulldog, and a frog

The tower of Nottingham Castle stood black against the evening sky. The Sheriff rode forth, followed by several mounted soldiers in shining chain mail. They drew a cart in their midst bearing Will Scarlet, his hands bound behind.

Will searched vainly for a familiar face along the way. When they had passed beyond the walls of the town, a tall man pushed through the crowd and climbed into the cart. It was Little John. Quickly he cut Will's bonds, and the two leaped away as the soldiers drew their swords.

dwarf's head, scythe, slice of pie

20   heads of a lizard and a bird, matchstick, shoe, snow shovel

Now Robin and all his men, clad as peasants and townsfolk, pressed in upon the mounted guards.

"Take them!" cried the Sheriff, who smote left and right with his sword. But Robin grasped the reins of the Sheriff's horse and twisted the weapon from his hand. He tossed it to Will Scarlet, saying, "The good Sheriff has lent you his sword!"

Robin's band cast aside their disguises. All now clashed swords with the soldiers, who had begun to disperse toward the town with cries for aid.

heads of a bear cub, a giraffe, and a lamb, dove, old woman's face, spoon

"Treason!" the Sheriff bellowed. But finally he turned his horse and spurred through the crowd. As he galloped past the town gates, a hail of arrows fell about him. Ringing in his ears was the triumphant laughter of Robin's band.

After an absence of many years, King Richard the Lion-Hearted returned to England. As he and his royal company approached the gates of Nottingham, trumpeters heralded their coming. People along the roads cheered as the armed knights with brilliant shields and painted lances passed on their mighty war horses. In the lead rode King Richard, a tall man with golden hair and beard and blue eyes.

padlock, leaf, hourglass, fly, heads of a jackal and a hound

gerbil, caterpillar, heads of a deer, an opossum, a vulture, and a rabbit   23

In the great hall of Nottingham Castle, knights, barons, and ladies feasted by torchlight. King Richard sat with the Sheriff at the table's head and heard many tales of the outlaw Robin Hood.

"I must somehow meet this rogue," said the King.

At dawn the next day King Richard rode out alone, clad as a simple wandering knight. When he came near Sherwood, a tall blond man stepped out from the trees.

"Hail, good knight," said Robin. "What do you seek?"

"I am weary and would find food and rest for the night," replied the King.

Robin bade the knight to follow him.

hat, slingshot, spade, open book, straw, needle

When they came to the place where Robin and his band dwelt, Robin said, "Let us first enjoy some sport."

While the men parried with the quarterstaff, the King marveled at their strength and laughed to see such spirited souls. Then a target was set across the clearing, and each man in turn lodged his arrow in the center.

The strange knight remarked aloud, "King Richard himself would be proud to have these warriors."

"We honor King Richard with our whole hearts," answered Robin.

bow tie, eyeglasses, clam, heads of a witch, a horse, and a tyrannosaurus

"Then hide no more as outlaws, for your King gladly pardons you all!" Saying this, the knight stood up and removed his hood of linked mail. Golden hair fell about his strong face.

"King Richard!" the men cried, and all knelt in homage.

The next day they all escorted Richard back to Nottingham, and never was one so vexed as the Sheriff when he saw his enemies greatly honored by the King.

Robin went straight to the home of Maid Marian. "At last I am free to walk openly again," he declared. She embraced him with joy, and they journeyed to Sherwood with light hearts.

Beneath a great spreading oak, Robin and Marian were wed by Friar Tuck, and the others honored them with merriment and song.

Robin lived happily with Marian and served the King honorably. After many years, Robin and Marian returned in peace to Sherwood Forest and walked again in the beauty of the silent trees.

It is told that, in his final hour, Robin lifted his faithful bow one last time. And with that arrow, his soul sped heavenward.

torch, dinosaur's head   **27**

You Found Them All?

Many years ago, King Richard the Lion-Hearted of England left his throne to fight in the Crusades. Those who ruled in his absence treated the people of the land unfairly.

During this time there lived in the country near Sherwood Forest an able-bodied youth named Robin Hood. While journeying one day to Nottingham, where he hoped to see his fair Maid Marian, Robin passed a group of foresters. Seeing his bow, they began to taunt him.

Robin became angry and foolishly wagered he could strike a deer in the distance. At this the men laughed, but Robin quickly drew his bow, and in seconds the stag lay still.

1: heads of a black panther, a zebra, and a troll, chickadee, saucer, scissors

"You have killed the King's deer!" the foresters cried. Realizing his mistake, Robin hastened toward the forest, but one of the men sent an arrow flying close by his ear. Robin turned and sped an answering shaft into the man's shoulder.

Thus did Robin Hood become an outlaw, and the Sheriff of Nottingham offered a high reward for his capture.

So Robin dwelt hidden in Sherwood Forest and greatly missed seeing Marian, for they had hoped to wed.

2: sailboat, baseball bat, sock, flute, horseshoe, parrot

There gathered about Robin other men who had been outlawed unjustly, among them valiant Will Scarlet. The men chose Robin for their chief. They fashioned clothing of dark green and built homes for themselves in the wild beauty of Sherwood.

Robin and his band won renown as skilled bowmen and brave fighters. They freely shared any goods they wrested from the rich and powerful with those who were oppressed.

3: light bulb, woodpecker, heads of a mouse, a collie, and a crow

One morning, as shafts of sunlight warmed the green moss, and birds filled the wood with their song, Robin set out alone.

His path led him to a great log spanning a deep, rushing stream. Approaching from the other side was a tall stranger. "Stand aside," called Robin, "while the better man crosses." "Then you must stand aside," answered the other, "for I am the better man."

4: heads of a goose and an ape, pointing hand, bat, fork, witch's hat

Noticing the strong staff the stranger held, Robin said, "Wait while I cut a staff to match yours."

Then both men stepped onto the log. As the water swirled below them, the two began to spar. Many a strong blow was parried by the other's staff. Robin dealt the stranger a whack on the ribs, but the stranger held his balance and swung his own staff squarely aside Robin's head.

Robin was hurled from the log, and he struck the water with a great splash.

5: snake, lizard, bird, knife, profile, wolf's head

As Robin surfaced, the stranger roared with laughter. Robin clambered upon the bank, all soaked and dripping with weeds, and laughed aloud at himself.

Then he raised his horn to his lips and sent forth a blast that echoed through the forest. Soon his green-clad men emerged from the shadows.

"Yonder stranger has given me a lesson in the cudgel I shall not forget," said Robin. "What is your name, friend?" "I am called John Little," replied the stranger. "I shall call you 'Little John' instead. I am Robin Hood. If you join our band, you will be my right-hand man and share our merry life in Sherwood."

6: mouse, arrow, pie, banana, dog's head, mushroom

The Sheriff of Nottingham, meanwhile, was plotting how he might capture Robin Hood. At last he sent messengers to every hamlet in the countryside, proclaiming a great shooting match to be held in Nottingham. Anyone who could draw a longbow was bidden to compete for the prize of a golden arrow. The Sheriff prepared his men to seize Robin should the outlaw be tempted to come show his skill.

7: hammer, rabbit, butterfly, boomerang, suitcase, funnel

When the day of the match arrived, merchants, pages, and knights with their ladies all gathered around the target range outside the town walls. On a raised seat beneath colored banners sat the Sheriff.

8: heads of an elephant and a chipmunk, folding knife, dragonfly, squirrel, axe

After the trumpets had sounded, each competitor shot in turn.

Then everyone laughed as a tattered beggar stepped forward with his bow. He was dressed in scarlet and wore a patch over one eye. Taking a shaft from his quiver, he looked over to Maid Marian. All fell silent as he drew his bow, held it a moment, and then released the arrow. Dead center it lodged as the onlookers stared in amazement.

"Receive your prize," grumbled the Sheriff when the beggar came before him. The scarlet stranger then walked over to Maid Marian and silently handed her the arrow. Their eyes met, and she nodded and smiled. He turned and walked boldly off the field.

9: hammer, heads of an eagle and a goose, broom, spoon, horn

That night the Sheriff sat at meat with his men. "I had expected to catch Robin Hood at the match today," he said. "But who was that insolent beggar who shot so well?" Just then an arrow flew through the window and lodged in the table with a thud. There was a scroll attached to its shaft. When the Sheriff read the note, he trembled with rage.

It read—

"Greetings to Your Grace, from Sherwood. You have given the prize to Robin Hood."

10: kite, mug, slice of bread, buckle, envelope, accordion

Several days later Robin wandered through the country dressed in chain mail with a sword by his side. On the banks of a wide stream, he came upon a stout friar.

"Ho," said Robin. "Would one so strong as you be willing to carry me across this stream? I would not have this steel tunic go to rust."

Chuckling to himself, the friar took Robin upon his back and stepped into the ford.

"Lest your sword get wet," said the friar, "I will carry it."

11: glove, fish, seal, heads of a baboon and a duck

When Robin had been deposited on the other shore, he asked for his sword. Then he saw the friar's own broadsword beneath his brown robe.

"I'll not return your sword unless you carry me back from whence we came," said the friar, the jolly man.

But while Robin waded across with the smiling friar on his back, he secretly unfastened the other's sword belt. So when the friar was set down, it was Robin who brandished both swords.

"Now," said Robin, "if you would have your own blade again, be kind enough to carry me over this stream."

12: heads of a cat, a lamb, and a donkey, wrench, arrowhead, cane

This time, when the friar had carried Robin to the center of the stream, he pitched him over his shoulders into the deepest water.

Then began an earnest duel between the two, their broadswords clashing together until the sun was low.

At that time Robin raised his horn, and shortly a dozen of his band came running from the trees. Then the friar blew upon his whistle, and four huge hounds burst from the thicket, with fangs bared.

13: pterodactyl, dog's head, duck, goldfish, spoon, pen

The good friar let forth peals of laughter as Robin and his men raced for the tallest trees.

"By the way," called Robin from his perch overhead, "I would be honored to have such a skilled swordsman in my band. I am Robin Hood."

"Good master! I have heard your name often. I am Friar Tuck." And with great apologies Friar Tuck called off his dogs as Robin descended the tree.

The friar gladly joined Robin's band that day.

14: feather, heart, drumstick, carrot, eel, lizard

The Sheriff was out hunting one evening when his path led him into Sherwood Forest. Suddenly he was surrounded by a dozen men in green and Robin Hood stepped forward.

"Noble Sheriff, surely you have journeyed here to enjoy our hospitality!"

They led his horse to their home beneath the tall trees. Then with merry smiles, they invited the grim-faced Sheriff to sit upon the moss. While the fires crackled, they served him the best fare they could muster and entertained him royally.

Robin said, "Before you return home, good Sheriff, we will gratefully accept your purse of gold."

15: crown, heads of a dog and a goat, trumpet, teacup, high-heeled shoe

When he had returned to Nottingham, the Sheriff called his men-at-arms together and demanded to have Robin Hood captured at any cost. Several groups of soldiers hid themselves in different parts of the forest.

Robin chose Will Scarlet to learn where they were hiding. Will ventured out at dawn in a monk's robe that covered his heavy sword. He soon found a group of the Sheriff's soldiers at a country inn.

16: hoe, shark, rake, hat, pail

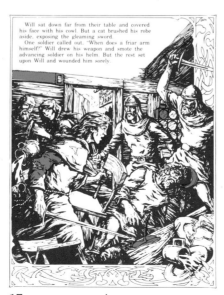

Will sat down far from their table and covered his face with his cowl. But a cat brushed his robe aside, exposing the gleaming sword.

One soldier called out, "When does a friar arm himself?" Will drew his weapon and smote the advancing soldier on his helm. But the rest set upon Will and wounded him sorely.

17: moon, saw, jump rope, grasshopper, giant's head, lantern

Robin was waiting for Will to return when he heard a horse pounding up the path toward him.

"Marian!" cried Robin. The lady reined in her horse where Robin stood.

"I had to come," she answered. "They have taken Will Scarlet to the Sheriff's castle and will hang him tomorrow!"

"Thank you," said Robin. "We will be there. But get you gone before the Sheriff's men see you here."

18: ladybug, salamander, bow, ring, pancake flipper, heads of a wolf, a bulldog, and a frog

The tower of Nottingham Castle stood black against the evening sky. The Sheriff rode forth, followed by several mounted soldiers in shining chain mail. They drew a cart in their midst bearing Will Scarlet, his hands bound behind.

Will searched vainly for a familiar face along the way. When they had passed beyond the walls of the town, a tall man pushed through the crowd and climbed into the cart. It was Little John. Quickly he cut Will's bonds, and the two leaped away as the soldiers drew their swords.

19: dwarf's head, scythe, slice of pie

20: heads of a lizard and a bird, matchstick, shoe, snow shovel

Now Robin and all his men, clad as peasants and townsfolk, pressed in upon the mounted guards.

"Take them!" cried the Sheriff, who smote left and right with his sword. But Robin grasped the reins of the Sheriff's horse and twisted the weapon from his hand. He tossed it to Will Scarlet, saying, "The good Sheriff hath lent you his sword!"

Robin's band cast aside their disguises. All now clashed swords with the soldiers, who had begun to disperse toward the town with cries for aid.

21: heads of a bear cub, a giraffe, and a lamb, dove, old woman's face, spoon

"Treason!" the Sheriff bellowed. But finally he turned his horse and spurred through the crowd. As he galloped past the town gates, a hail of arrows fell about him. Ringing in his ears was the triumphant laughter of Robin's band.

After an absence of many years, King Richard the Lion-Hearted returned to England. As he and his royal company approached the gates of Nottingham, trumpeters heralded their coming. People along the roads cheered as the armed knights with brilliant shields and painted lances passed on their mighty war horses. In the lead rode King Richard, a tall man with golden hair and beard and blue eyes.

22: padlock, leaf, hourglass, fly, heads of a jackal and a hound

23: gerbil, caterpillar, heads of a deer, an opossum, a vulture, and a rabbit

In the great hall of Nottingham Castle, knights, barons, and ladies feasted by torchlight. King Richard sat with the Sheriff at the table's head and heard many tales of the outlaw Robin Hood.

"I must somehow meet this rogue," said the King.

At dawn the next day King Richard rode out alone, clad as a simple wandering knight. When he came near Sherwood, a tall blond man stepped out from the trees.

"Hail, good knight," said Robin. "What do you seek?"

"I am weary and would find food and rest for the night," replied the King.

Robin bade the knight to follow him.

24: hat, slingshot, spade, open book, straw, needle

When they came to the place where Robin and his band dwelt, Robin said, "Let us first enjoy some sport."

While the men parried with the quarterstaff, the King marveled at their strength and laughed to see such spirited souls. Then a target was set across the clearing, and each man in turn lodged his arrow in the center.

The strange knight remarked aloud, "King Richard himself would be proud to have these warriors."

"We honor King Richard with our whole hearts," answered Robin.

25: bow tie, eyeglasses, clam, heads of a witch, a horse, and a tyrannosaurus

"Then hide no more as outlaws, for your King gladly pardons you all!" Saying this, the knight stood up and removed his hood of linked mail. Golden hair fell about his strong face.

"King Richard!" the men cried, and all knelt in homage.

The next day they all escorted Richard back to Nottingham, and never was one so vexed as the Sheriff when he saw his enemies so greatly honored by the King.

Robin went straight to the home of Maid Marian. "At last I am free to walk openly again," he declared. She embraced him with joy, and they journeyed to Sherwood with light hearts.

26: crutch, crayon, the letter **A,** faucet, ant, paintbrush, snail, bell, lion's head

Beneath a great spreading oak, Robin and Marian were wed by Friar Tuck, and the others honored them with merriment and song.

Robin lived happily with Marian and served the King honorably. After many years, Robin and Marian returned in peace to Sherwood Forest and walked again in the beauty of the silent trees.

It is told that, in his final hour, Robin lifted his faithful bow one last time. And with that arrow, his soul sped heavenward.

27: torch, dinosaur's head